Things I Like

I Like Horses

By Meg Gaertner

level 1
little blue readers

www.littlebluehousebooks.com

Copyright © 2020 by Little Blue House, Mendota Heights, MN 55120. All rights reserved. No part of this book may be reproduced or utilized in any form or by any means without written permission from the publisher.

Little Blue House is distributed by North Star Editions:
sales@northstareditions.com | 888-417-0195

Produced for Little Blue House by Red Line Editorial.

Photographs ©: gorillaimages/Shutterstock Images, cover; bjdlzx/iStockphoto, 4, 16 (top right); Asia Images/iStockphoto, 7, 16 (top left); Vasyl Syniuk/Shutterstock Images, 8–9; wavebreakmedia/Shutterstock Images, 11, 16 (bottom right); Antonio_Diaz/iStockphoto, 13; Fotokostic/Shutterstock Images, 14–15; Diane Bliessen/iStockphoto, 16 (bottom left)

Library of Congress Control Number: 2019908613

ISBN
978-1-64619-013-3 (hardcover)
978-1-64619-052-2 (paperback)
978-1-64619-091-1 (ebook pdf)
978-1-64619-130-7 (hosted ebook)

Printed in the United States of America
Mankato, MN
012020

About the Author

Meg Gaertner enjoys reading, writing, dancing, and being outside. She lives in Minnesota.

Table of Contents

I Like Horses 5

Glossary 16

Index 16

horse

I Like Horses

I like horses.

I pet the horse.

I like horses.

I feed the horse.

7

I like horses.

I brush the horse.

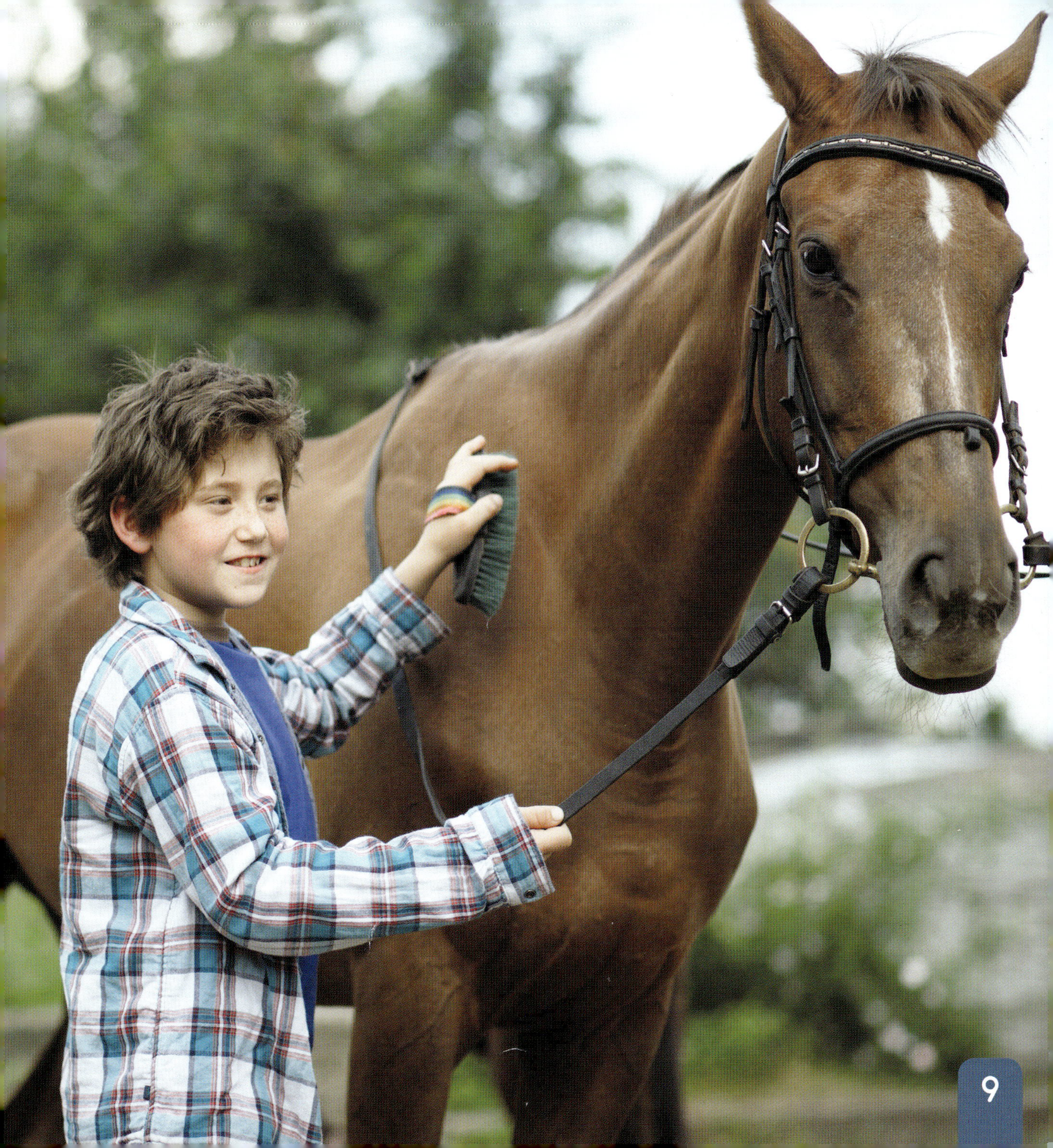

I like horses.

I saddle the horse.

11

I like horses.

I sit on the horse.

13

I like horses.

I ride the horse.

15

Glossary

feed

pet

horse

saddle

Index

B
brush, 8

F
feed, 6

R
ride, 14

S
saddle, 10